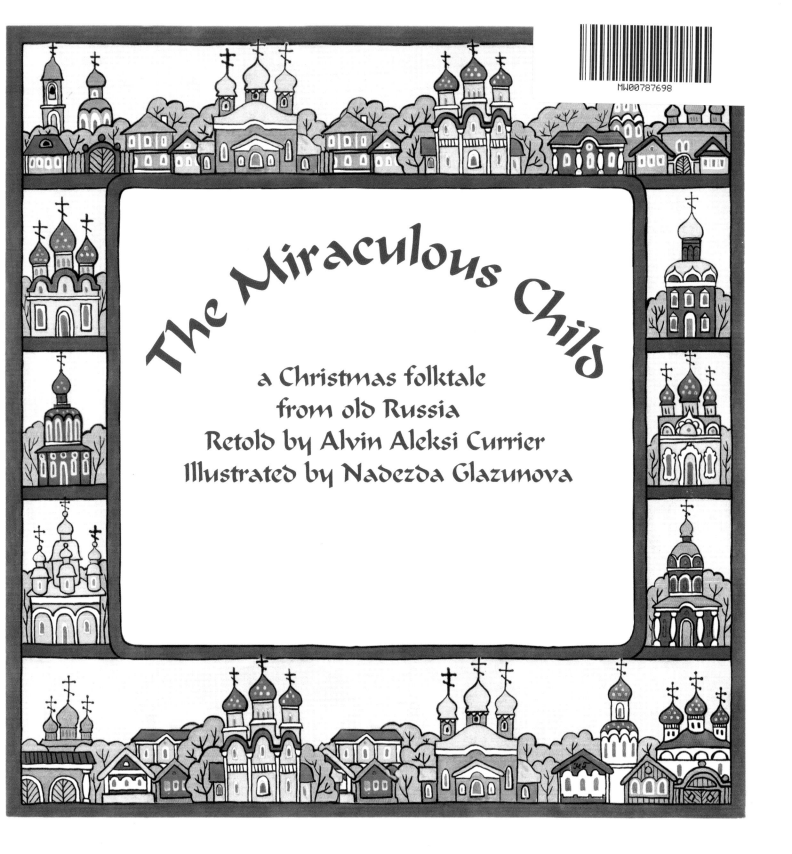

The Miraculous Child

a Christmas folktale
from old Russia
Retold by Alvin Aleksi Currier
Illustrated by Nadezda Glazunova

The Miraculous Child

Text copyright © by Alvin Alexsi Currier
Illustrations copyright © by Nadezda Glazunova

Published by Conciliar Press
P.O. Box 76, Ben Lomond, California
Printed in China
All Rights Reserved.

ISBN 10: 1-888212-20-9
ISBN 13: 978-1888212-20-4

FOREWORD

Few phrases conjure more powerful magic than the simple words, "Once upon a time:" for this formula announces a story and stories are the life blood of every people. Among the stories at the heart of the lands of the Christian cultures none is better known, or more deeply loved, than the few biblical verses that tell the story of the birth of a child. This humble Christmas story annually inspires countless versions and variations of itself, embellished by pageants, poetry, and music. The themes of Christmas are not only well known, they are well loved and deeply rooted. The tale here belongs to the folk tradition of Russia, retold by Grandparent to grandchild, across generations. The plot is simple and the theme is familiar. The power is in the haunting tones and the rich Orthodox colors of humble faith.

Alvin Alexsi Currier
St. Paul, Minnesota, USA
Pascha 2000

The Miraculous Child

Once upon a Christmastime
in old Russia
in a humble log home
at the end of a trail
that turned off the road
that passed by the very last village,
deep in the woods,
far, far from the town,
there lived a poor woodcutter
with his mother, his wife and his children.
Inside he worked on this cold winter day,
lacing birch-bark buckets.
And as he worked away
he did silently pray
for his heart was filled with sadness.
Early this year the cold had come,
the wind, the snow, and the darkness,
and now there was little left to eat
and nothing left to trade or sell,
nothing for the Christmas feast.
The baby cried,
the children played,
the poor man worked
and worked
and prayed.

In the flickering light
in the long winter night,
the woodcutter worked as he prayed,
and when depressed, he stopped to rest,
he stared at the mess
that was scattered all around him.
There lay what he'd fashioned by his hand
in the tradition of his land,
simple birch bark buckets.
Everyone used such humble containers
for storing this, and keeping that
safe from ants, the mice or a rat.
Slowly a warmth filled the woodcutter's heart
and a smile appeared on his face,
as he sensed indeed
God had given heed,
and he saw how his prayer had been answered.
For wasn't it true
that for buckets like these
there was always a need,
which meant they might also be traded.
The hope was dim,
the chance was slim,
but now he knew what he must do.
He packed up his work,
hitched his horse to the sleigh,
and headed off to the town
at the first light of day.

Up the trail and onto the road,
past villages, churches, fields, and farms,
singing away, he drove his sleigh
onward, on to the town.
There were people there from everywhere,
and wondrous things for sale.
There were satins and silk and a samovar,
wines and meats and caviar,
but all the day
as time ticked away,
no one came seeking for birch-bark buckets.
Until at last, a baker came by,
and the woodcutter's work caught his eye,
so he offered a trade
and a deal was made,
and the poor man at least
had bread for the feast.

It wasn't much;
it was precious little,
this loaf that made him so happy,
but they hadn't had any bread to eat
since a month ago when they ran out of wheat,
so this loaf was for them
really a treat.
In the setting sun
he hurried along,
humming a song,
when suddenly in the oncoming night
he glimpsed in the dusk
an unbelievable sight.
Out in a field, under a tree,
there sat on a stump
a little boy shivering and cold.
Astonished, the woodcutter reined in his horse,
jumped from his sled,
and rushed through the snow.
"Holy God!" he prayed
as he drew near,
"What on earth
is happening here?"
Yet never did he hesitate
as he slipped off his coat,
wrapped up the boy,
and carried him back to his sleigh.

The dark settled in,
the stars came out,
and the night grew bitter and cold.
The owl looked on from the old oak tree,
and the rabbit hopped out of his hole to see
the wondrous sight that was passing.
A man in his shirt
stayed strangely warm
as he raced along,
bearing his precious bundle.
The whip did crack and the sleigh bells jingled,
as the pines peeked out of their coats of snow
to watch them come
and watch them go.
When passing a church the bells did ring
and others claim
the stars did sing,
as under the twinkling heavenly host
the racing sled did silently coast.
Through the last village
at last they flew,
skimmed over the field,
plunged into the wood,
and finally came
to the woodcutter's cottage and clearings.

Warmly his family welcomed the boy
and wrapped him quick
in a feather tick,
and tucked him in bed
on top of the old stone oven.
He spoke not a peep
but fell fast asleep, as down below
in the candle glow
the family prepared
for the Christ Child's birth,
for peace on earth,
for the Holy Nativity feast.
When all was just right
and the tree was alight,
they gathered him down
and ringed him around,
to sing holy prayers for their Christmas.

When the prayers were said, they cut the bread,
and the first slice they gave to the stranger.
His eyes filled with tears
as he looked at them all,
and his silence he broke
as softly he spoke,
and this is what he said:

> "When the poor share what little they have,
>   with another who's poor and has nothing,
>   God's heart grows warm,
>   God's eyes grow moist,
>   and God's tear falls to earth
>   with a blessing."

All were silent at this saying,
and none could grasp its meaning.

So the woodcutter's wife
continued to slice
the wonderful feastday loaf.
She gave a piece to her baby boy,
and then with joy
another she gave to her firstborn son.
Two more she cut for her daughters two
and one for her dearest Babushka.
But as she cut and as she sliced,
all sitting there
became aware
of a miracle appearing.
She cut and cut the holy bread,
but it didn't matter how many she fed:
the loaf refused to get smaller.
All eyes filled with wonder.
Some trembled with awe.
Grandma invoked the Holy Name
while they ate,
and ate,
and ate,
but the loaf stayed the same.

Then on that silent sacred eve,
in that dark and tiny cottage room,
the holy night
with a brilliance of light
was slowly,
slowly flooded.
And there where the little boy had sat,
he now as an angel appeared.
He spoke not a word,
yet choirs were heard
as in dazzling light,
that holy night,
his fingers he formed
in sacred design,
and moving his hand
in flowing strokes
he signed the cross
and laid on that house
his blessing.
In a second's space
he hallowed the place,
and just as fast
all was past,
and into the dark
he disappeared.

To this day, if you pass this way,
you will still feel the power of that blessing.
For ever since
in the woodcutter's life,
with his farm, his family, and his beloved wife,
in years that are good,
and in times that are harsh,
all has gone well
as they are quick to tell,
since that night of the angel's appearing.
And to this day, if you pass this way,
there is another sight worth seeing.
It is a rustic bench,
as Papa points out,
where nobody sits or is seated.
It's a holy place,
and the reason for that
is because
it is where
an angel
sat.

Do not neglect to show hospitality to strangers, for thereby some have entertained angels unaware. Hebrews 13:2

About the Illustrator

Nadezda Glazunova began her artistic career in her native Russia by painting floral designs on the mass-produced products of a communist souvenir factory. Her obvious talent won her admission to the National College of Traditional and Folk Art, where she studied such masters as Ivan Bilibin, and met her husband, Leonid, a master woodcarver. After graduation they made their home in Petrozavodsk, working together as artists. In 1990 Nadezda received her first commission, which was to design religious Christmas and Easter cards in response to need created by the fall of communism. Since those first cards were printed in Vienna, Austria, in 1991 her cards have had a continuous market in Europe and America.

Working with Alvin Alexsi Currier, this book was published in German and English in Vienna in 1995. This first small edition sold out almost immediately. *Alyosha's Apple*, a second book from this team, was published in 1999 and has made possible the new layout and printing of this edition in English and Romanian.

Nadezda's work, full of color, life, and joy, reflects her longing for her beloved country to return to the kind of life, rooted in the faith and traditions of Orthodoxy, that she depicts in her paintings. Today she lives with her husband and son in a humble wooden home near to the golden-domed monastery of the Holy Trinity in Sergiyev Posad, in Russia.

About the Author

Outwardly Alvin Alexsi Currier is known as a son of the city of Minneapolis, and until his retirement after 35 years, he was classified professionally as a Presbyterian clergyman who served various midwestern American churches, two parishes in Germany, and for eleven years as a college chaplain.

Inwardly he is a pilgrim who, sensing his spiritual emptiness, fled professional life for the forest in 1975. There in the following two decades he lived a semi-monastic life, founding and tending St. Herman's Hermitage as a place of prayer for all people, and finding his spiritual home in the Orthodox Church.

Today with his wife Anastasia he lives in St. Paul, Minnesota, as an author, artist, and interpreter of Orthodoxy, traveling widely in Eastern Europe and organizing pilgrimages of mutual encouragement for others to experience Orthodoxy from the inside out. His other books include: *Karelia: An Introduction to, and Meditation on, Karelian Orthodox Culture*, *Alyosha's Apple*, and *How the Monastery Came to Be on Top of the Mountain*.